Old Tom's
Big Book of Beauty

PLEASE WASH
YOUR HANDS
BEFORE YOU READ ME
AND KEEP ME CLEAN

Leigh HOBBS

BLOOMSBURY

LONDON BERLIN NEW YORK

For my mother Gwen,
who did her best

Bloomsbury Publishing, London, Berlin and New York

First published in Great Britain in May 2010 by Bloomsbury Publishing Plc
36 Soho Square, London, W1D 3QY

First published by Allen & Unwin Pty Ltd, Sydney, Australia

Old Tom's Big Book of Beauty copyright © Leigh Hobbs 2007
The moral right of the author/illustrator has been asserted

A CIP catalogue record of this book is available from the British Library

ISBN 978 1 4088 0523 7

1 3 5 7 9 10 8 6 4 2

Printed in China by Toppan Leefung Printing Ltd, Dongguan, Guangdong

Cover design by Leigh Hobbs & Sandra Nobes
Text design by Sandra Nobes

All papers used by Bloomsbury Publishing are natural, recyclable products
made from wood grown in well-managed forests. The manufacturing processes
conform to the environmental regulations of the country of origin

www.bloomsbury.com/childrens
www.leighhobbs.com.au

Angela Throgmorton had always adored Old Tom, though even when he was a baby she had a feeling there was room for improvement.

So, when he was a bit more grown up, Angela gave him a gift.
It was a book, *The Big Book of Beauty*.

Angela was thrilled when Old Tom read it from cover to cover.
It wasn't long before she noted some changes.

For a start, Old Tom always
seemed to be in the bathroom…

splashing, drying

and brushing.

She could hear him
            whooshing, gargling,
                        combing, cleaning
                                    and preening.

Old Tom was certainly taking an interest in his appearance.
'Let's hope it lasts!' thought Angela Throgmorton.

the
EL NATURALE

the SHOCKER

the FURBALL

the
FURBALL SURPRISE

the FABULOUS

the SHOW-OFF

Old Tom was keen to have
a stylish new look,
and *The Big Book of Beauty*
was full of ideas.

The Shocker was Old Tom's favourite for shopping,
whereas the Furball...

felt just *fabulous* for afternoon tea with Angela's friends.

But alas it wasn't only Old Tom's appearance that was changing.

Soon Old Tom's diary was so full that Angela
had to ring for an appointment.
There was no time at all to help with the housework.
Old Tom had beauty creams to apply…

and strawberry-flavoured milk baths for his delicate complexion.
Angela was tempted to take back *The Big Book of Beauty*.
She had a feeling…

The Big Book of Beauty had gone to Old Tom's head.

'Perhaps it's a stage he's going through,'
thought Angela Throgmorton.
Whatever it was, she was seeing less and less of him.

Though one day she caught a glimpse
on her way home with the groceries.

And once, Angela spotted Old Tom at the Beauty Parlour.
Another time, on the bus, he pretended not to see her.

More and more, Old Tom was mixing with a different crowd.
He went to the Opera and sang along in his splendid new suit.

Old Tom was seen at party after party.

He never waited to be invited.

Meanwhile, he was treating Angela's house like a hotel.

Of course, he still came home for meals, to relax, to check
his diary and to take a look at *The Big Book of Beauty*.
'A pity he missed the section on good manners,'
thought Angela Throgmorton.

Angela longed for her old Old Tom.
Nowadays, she had to make do
with late-night peeks while
he enjoyed his beauty sleep,

or with a picture or two
in the social pages.

He was often on the evening news.
In fact Old Tom seemed to be everywhere …

at openings, closings,
a ship launch
and even at the races.

However, Old Tom was wearing out his welcome.
After some fancy footwork while ballroom dancing,
he was shown the door.

Then, when his fleas went wild at the Beauty Parlour,
Old Tom was thrown out…

and told never to return.

Worse still, at a rather important event,
Old Tom forgot himself and put his foot in the cheese dip.

Soon *someone* was feeling unwelcome EVERYWHERE.

Old Tom had ignored the one who loved him most.

By now Angela knew that *The Big Book of Beauty* had been a great big mistake.

For Old Tom had always been perfect, just as he was.

Well, he was certainly as beautiful as he was ever going to get.